WITH A STAR in MY HAND

MARGARITA ENGLE

WITH A STAR in MY HAND

RUBÉN DARÍO, POETRY HERO

Atheneum   New York London Toronto Sydney New Delhi

ACKNOWLEDGMENTS

I thank God for poetry.

I am grateful to my husband and the rest of our family,
especially my mother, who taught me to love poetry.

Special thanks to the memory of my *abuelita* Fefa
and *bisabuelita* Ana Dominga for their reverence for poetry, especially Rubén Darío's.
I am grateful to Carol Zapata-Whelan, Emily Aguilo-Pérez, Alma Flor Ada,
Isabel Campoy, David Rojas, and Claire Annette Noland.

Profound gratitude to my agent, Michelle Humphrey;
my wonderful editor, Reka Simonsen;
and the whole Atheneum publishing team.

atheneum

An imprint of Simon & Schuster Children's Publishing Division
1230 Avenue of the Americas, New York, New York 10020
This book is a work of fiction. Any references to historical events, real people,
or real places are used fictitiously. Other names, characters, places, and events
are products of the author's imagination, and any resemblance to actual
events or places or persons, living or dead, is entirely coincidental.
Text copyright © 2020 by Margarita Engle
Jacket illustration copyright © 2020 by Willian Santiago
All rights reserved, including the right of reproduction
in whole or in part in any form.
Atheneum logo is a trademark of Simon & Schuster, Inc.
For information about special discounts for bulk purchases,
please contact Simon & Schuster Special Sales at 1-866-506-1949
or business@simonandschuster.com.
The Simon & Schuster Speakers Bureau can bring authors to your live event. For
more information or to book an event, contact the Simon & Schuster Speakers
Bureau at 1-866-248-3049 or visit our website at www.simonspeakers.com.
Book design by Debra Sfetsios-Conover
The text for this book was set in ITC Legacy Serif Std.
Manufactured in the United States of America
First Edition
10 9 8 7 6 5 4 3 2 1
Library of Congress Cataloging-in-Publication Data
Names: Engle, Margarita, author.
Title: With a star in my hand : Rubén Darío, poetry hero / Margarita Engle.
Description: First edition. | New York : Atheneum Books for Young Readers,
[2020] | Summary: A novel in verse about the life and work of Rubén Darío,
a Nicaraguan poet who started life as an abandoned child and grew to
become the father of a new literary movement. Includes historical notes. |
Includes bibliographical references.
Identifiers: LCCN 2019003842 | ISBN 9781534424937 (hardcover) |
ISBN 9781534424951 (eBook)
Subjects: LCSH: Darío, Rubén, 1867–1916—Childhood and youth—Juvenile
fiction. | Nicaragua—History—1838–1909—Fiction. | CYAC: Novels in verse. |
Darío, Rubén, 1867–1916—Childhood and youth—Fiction. | Poets—Fiction. |
Nicaragua—History—1937–1979—Fiction.
Classification: LCC PZ7.5.E54 Rub 2020 | DDC [Fic]—dc23
LC record available at https://lccn.loc.gov/2019003842

For Alma Flor Ada and Isabel Campoy,
heroes of bilingual literature;
and for all the heroic poets of the future

¡Momotombo se alzaba lírico y soberano,
yo tenía quince años: una estrella en la mano!

Momotombo rose up lyrical and free,
I was fifteen years old: a star in my hand!
—Rubén Darío

ABANDONED

My first memory was one I could not understand
until years later: playing with towering animals
under a palm tree, all around me gentle eyes,
feathery green fronds,
and sticky tidbits of fruit
stuck to cow lips.

The cattle were smelly
and friendly,
just as hungry
for palm fruit
as I was
for milk.

Where did Mamá go?
I was too young for a sense of time,
but somehow I expected to be exiled forever
in that musical tangle of thumping hoofs
and clackety horns, my own wailing voice
adding a flutelike magic
to the noise.

LOST

When I remember abandonment,
all I feel is a sense of my smallness.

The roaming bulls ignored me.
I must have been too tiny
to seem
truly human.

Muddy legs, grubby face.
If I'd stayed in that cow world
long enough, I might have grown
hoofs, horns,
two more legs,
and a swishing tail.

WILD RHYMES

Jaguars, pumas, and other big cats,
poisonous snakes and vampire bats . . .

when Mamá abandoned me in a jungle,
did she think about all the fearful creatures
or was she merely offering me a green gift,
the sneaky hunt
for shy
sly
strangely
prowling
rhymes
to help me pass safely
through a dangerous
wilderness
called
time?

AM I AN ANIMAL YET?

With the rhythmic music of the herd
rattling through my busy mind,
I tried to moo like a cow,
coo like a dove,
then holler
and bellow,
just a lost and lonely little boy
whose human voice rose up
in an effort to transform
beastly
emotions.

No, I was not an animal,
but yes, I felt grateful
to four-legged creatures
for the lullabies they sang
to green trees
and blue sky.

Someday I will sing too,
instead of moaning.

FOUND

My mother's friend found me.
He was an angry farmer who spanked
my bottom.
Thwack!
Smack!
The crackling shuffle of rustling hoofs
sounded like a dance, as my cow friends
saw their chance to escape, leaving me alone
with the shouting stranger
who tossed me across
a mule's broad back,
where I bumped and swayed
all the way
to a palm-thatched hut . . .

but Mamá was not there
in the little house.
She had gone
    away.

LIKE A BIRD

Black eyes.
Slender hands.
Dark hair.
Waterfall laughter.

Trying to picture
my lost mother
has become a race
of entrancing words
that gallop
faster
and faster.

Did Mamá fly into the sky
like a winged being,
or is she alive
and hiding?

BIG MOUTH

A bearded man on a spirited horse
rescued me from the gloomy farmer.

We thundered far across the green hills
of Honduras, hoofbeats making me feel
like a centaur, as we galloped over the border
to Nicaragua—my homeland—but not
to the small room in the back of a store
in the little town of Metapa
where I was born.

Instead, we ended up in a rambling old
horseshoe-shaped house in the city of León,
where I was finally told that Mamá wanted me
to live HERE
with strangers.

I soon learned that the bearded rescuer
was my great-uncle, called El Bocón
by all who knew him.

Big Mouth, such a suitable nickname
for a man who tells tall tales
in a booming, larger-than-life
story voice.

He speaks of steep mountains with icy peaks,
and of gallant knights who battle ogres and dragons,
and of smoothly rolling hills in distant lands,
countries so remote
and amazing
that I can hardly absorb
the fascinating range
of exotic names.

Has he really traveled so much?
France? California?

Soon, when I grow up,
I plan to roam the earth
and be a Big Mouth too,
speaking truthfully
whenever I choose,
never caring
if anyone
is offended.

Any harsh fact is so much better
than telling lies like a tricky mother
who pretends
she'll just be gone
for a little while.

ADOPTED

El Bocón and his wife,
my great-aunt Bernarda,
decide to make me their son.

He's huge and loud, she's small and flowery,
with curly hair, a delicate voice,
and an eager way of making children
join all her songs, parties,
and prayers.

Living in their vast, echoing home,
I soon learn the essential skill of storytelling
along with horsemanship, hunting, fishing,
and wild fruit harvesting.

The only art I never master
is convincing others that I don't really care
how
and why
Mamá vanished.

SO MANY STORYTELLERS

The city is musical
with church bells
and chirping birds,
heels tapping
on cobblestones,
and lush green gardens
that grow so fast that every morning
brings new blossoms, each with its own
enchanted fragrance.

El Bocón is not the only one who fills
the humid air
with ribbons of words
that seem to draw pictures. . . .

Serapia is the cook who tells tales she learned
from her *africano* ancestors, and Goyo the gardener
speaks of our shared native heritage,
my brown skin and black hair
just as *indio* as his.

Was Mamá a *mestiza* of half-Matagalpan descent,
or did she belong to the Pipil Nahua,
Maya, Chontal, Niquirano, Chorotega,
Miskito, or some other proud forest nation?

When I sit in church, the stories I hear
are even more improbable than El Bocón's
fanciful tales of foreign lands.

The priest speaks of a man
swallowed by a fish,
a boy with a slingshot
who battles a giant,
burning bushes,
and a talking donkey—but no one
ever mentions children left behind
in cow pastures, so maybe reality
is the strangest,
most mystery-filled
terrible
true story
of all.

MY NAME IS A STATUE,
BUT MY MIND ROAMS FREE

I almost melt in the church's smoky heat,
where a scented mist of incense rises,
cradling murmured words
as we sing all together,
before stepping out
into the blaze of sunlight.

Tía Bernarda leads me across the scorching plaza,
and when I complain, I'm lifted by the strong arms
of Serapia, but I'm too big to be carried
like a baby, so I squirm free, using my liberty
to gaze into the eyes of a marble horseman
who is said to be my godfather Félix, the man
who gave me his name
and who would have adopted me
if he hadn't died and turned into stone.

Does everyone who has ever been alive
end up motionless in a peaceful park
sooner or later?

Apparently yes, because before I know
what has happened, there goes El Bocón too,
buried in the graveyard
under a headstone
without any clear explanation

other than Serapia's quiet sigh,
as she says *así pasa con los viejos*—
that's what happens to the old.

If life is a story
about the passing of time,
I think God should make
all the sad parts
rhyme.

HOME

Without my great-uncle
we're suddenly poor,
so the dusty old rooms
and orchard-like courtyard
should feel solemn and silent, but no—
Serapia continues to chatter as she cooks,
and Goyo still weaves legends while he weeds
between fruit trees.

Serene moments are spent reading
under the *jícaro* gourd tree, beside *la granada*,
the pomegranate with ruby-red seeds
that offer such a messy adventure,
their brilliant hue
one of glittering gems
in a pirate's treasure chest,
the taste making me think of distance—a ship
sailing off into the sunset, my hands so juicy
that a few pages of each precious book
end up stained, as if the story has absorbed
bright light from my own glowing
daydreams.

MY TREE FRIENDS

The trunk of the *jícaro* is black,
its leaves small and feathery,
the gourds dry and useful,
each one a big
wingless bird shape
that can be carved into a bowl
or musical instrument.

The pomegranate is beautiful too,
with its gnarled wood, and jewel-like fruit.

When I sit down to read in the shade
of tree friends, I see a row of hammocks
and rocking chairs, but I prefer earth,
the natural home of growing roots
and rhymed verses.

NIGHT

By daylight, I love the outdoors garden-heart
at the center of this vast house, but after dark
even the bedrooms
are scary.

Bernarda's old mother tells stories of horror.

Serapia and Goyo share ghostly tales too.

Owls rustle and call from up above on the roof.

Mice scurry
from corner
to corner
like four-footed
messengers
of terror.

If only I could forget Mamá's disappearance.

It would be so much easier to fall asleep
peacefully.

CHANGING NAMES

I have always been Félix Rubén García Sarmiento,
but now Bernarda no longer wants me to carry
the name of my godfather—that motionless
marble statue
in the park.

Suddenly, I am expected to think of myself
as Rubén Darío.

It's a change so strange
that it feels like just one more eerie story,
as if my old self is suddenly
ghostly.

Félix meant happy, lucky, blessed.
Rubén simply means look, it's a son—but I'm not
the real son of this house, just a substitute,
the nephew, more trouble
than I'm worth.

FRIGHTENED BY GROWN-UPS

The stories told by adults
are about a hairy hand
that walks the streets at night
like a spider,
and a headless priest
who wanders all over the city,
and a witch with cruel laughter,
and ordinary people who fly away
high above rooftops.

Whenever the smell of sulfur
rises and pours down over this house,
I want to believe that it's just the odor
of bathwater in a volcanic hot springs,
but old people
keep warning me
about fiery lava
and other
volcanic
evils.

LIGHTNESS

Pesadillas—heavy nightmares,
the weight of rude questions
from visitors who ask
why my mother
left me.

This happens almost every evening
at *las tertulias*, Bernarda's lively gatherings
of shopkeepers and other gossiping adults.

Curious grown-ups should know
that furious orphans don't have any answers
to questions about wandering parents.

So I lie down
    wounded
        by words
and wake up
    with nosebleeds
        headaches
            fears

but words are also my sturdy refuge
by day, in merciful sunlight, beneath
the gourd tree,
beside the pomegranate.

So I read, in the morning,
after each nightmare—
soothing poems,
glowing adventure stories,
and radiant tales
of not-quite-rhymed
poetic wishes.

SCHOOL

I taught myself to read when I was three,
but now there are teachers to add confusion,
sometimes a poet who spanks me
for reciting rhymes out of turn,
and at other times a gentle *india*,
a woman
who bakes cookies
and refuses to punish
anyone.

Don Quixote, the Bible, horror tales, and comedies—
I never grow tired of exploring the endless variety
of natural and supernatural stories.

Math, geography, and grammar
also have their orderly place in my school day,
but poetry arrives in its own way,
wild like a hurricane,
a storm of turbulent wind
and ocean waves!

FIRST VERSES

The sisters of the bishop sell candies
in the shapes of birds and animals,
treats so delicious that I learn
to trade skillfully rhymed words
about those sweet creations
for sugary treasures,
which I gobble
with pleasure.

Sometimes the sisters
show off my poems
about doves and lambs
to other children,
as examples of work
that deserves a reward,
but I don't think of poetry
as labor, when each rhyme
about a parrot
or a panther
is so much
fun!

A BURST OF VERSES!

During Easter week, the streets
are decorated with arches
made from branches, green cascades
of coconut fronds and banana leaves,
along with blossoms from *el corozo,*
the vegetable ivory palm tree
that has pale-hearted nuts
I can carve
into tiny statuettes
of hummingbirds,
the wings just as smooth and white
as real elephant tusks.

Feathers, ribbons, and strands of colorful paper,
cut into all sorts of complicated, lacy shapes.

The street in front of our house looks like a toy store
imagined, and then brought to life by a magician.

On the ground, there are carpets of pictures
made by artists who work with sawdust—
red cedar, mahogany, yellow *mora,* black ebony,
and on top of those fragments of tumbled forest,
a rainbow of flower petals, wheat grains,
corn, beans, and other seeds, as if to praise
this generous earth

for a wealth
of delicious growth.

I stand outdoors
dazzled by brilliant designs,
especially the one that dangles right in front of my
astonished eyes, a golden pomegranate
instead of a natural, ruby-red fruit.

Has a clever artist coated this *granada*
with some sort of glittering metallic dust?

Is it real gold?
When I reach up to touch
the shimmering sculpture,
it cracks open, and a shower of paper
rains down—verses, poems, all written
by me, the ones I traded for candy!

Are my scraps of rhyme
really so valuable
that the bishop's sisters
want to share them
with everyone?

Maybe all I'll ever need
for the rest of my life
is this thunderous comfort,
my own wild storm
of explosive
poetry!

READING, READING, READING

There is only one way to improve my chime of verses.
So I read, read, read, all the carefully rhymed words
written long before
I ever existed.

PRACTICING TRADITIONAL
POETIC FORMS

I am determined to write a perfect *redondilla*
of four eight-syllable lines, with the rhyme pattern
a b b a.

I try all sorts of formal rhymes,	a
first a four-line *redondilla,*	b
then a brave five-line *quintilla,*	b
until I'm rhyming all the time.	a

CHALLENGING MYSELF

Next, I scribble an old-fashioned *octavilla*
of two *redondillas*, using the familiar
rhyme pattern
a b b a   a c c a.

Poetry keeps flooding my mind.	a
Soon I try long *octavillas*	b
of two attached *redondillas*	b
with rhymes that can be hard to find.	a

Once all the words have been entwined	a
I see the pleasure of knowing	c
that a poem can change, growing	c
beyond old forms with counted lines.	a

WHY I BEGIN TO CRAVE
IMPROVISATION

Décimas are sets of two *redondillas*
linked by a two-line bridge of eight syllables each
with a rhyme pattern
a b b a   a c   a c c a,
and *espinelas* are the same
only ending with
c d d c.

Seguidillas have alternating lines of five
and seven syllables, with vowel rhymes
anywhere in the even lines (2, 4, 6), instead of
always appearing at the ends,
perfectly aligned . . .

so I start to experiment with changing everything
and just letting verses flow, finding their way
into musical rhythms that dance on natural air
tempest-tossed,
wind-driven!

Why obey such strict rhyming rules
when poems have minds, hearts, and souls
of their own, always loving
freedom?

VOWEL RHYMES

I love
to rhyme
just the insides
of syllables
sometimes.

This is still a verse
even though the words
seem to hold internal mysteries,
these assonantal vowel rhymes that can be found
anywhere in a line, not just at the end
so rigidly
final.

EVERY SADNESS

Lost mother.
Dead father.

Even the smallest
stormy poem
offers enough
nearly rhymed
room
for all
human
sorrows.

Yes, I'm angry.
So I fill my verses with beautiful swans
and peacocks, hoping the reader will understand
that this contrast with hideous ugliness
lies at the heart of my rage, because
I feel cheated
by abandonment
and other human
cruelties.

SHARED SORROWS

With so much fury
disguised inside glorious verses,
I become the object of adult attention.

Families ask me to write poems for them to read
at the funerals of loved ones.

My windstorm of rhythms, both rhymed
and nearly rhymed, turns into a strange
sort of musical wealth, that I must spend
to help others, even when each furious
burst
of verses
hurts
my wounded heart
and suffering
mind.

ANY HAPPINESS

Every Sunday, my family
celebrates a children's dance, with aunts,
uncles, cousins, and other festive relatives.

Some of my *tías* seem a bit crazy,
all wrapped up in ruffles and wearing
shiny red shoes, as if they think they
are still little girls
like their pretty daughters.

These dressed-up aunts claim to be impressed
with my elaborate, rhythmic sonnets
written for funerals, so now I'm invited
to recite completely new rhymes
for female cousins, *las primas*,
generous girls who are eager to praise
my poetic talent, as long as their names
are included in the titles of verses.

I scribble on fans and in autograph albums,
my hurricane of words always inspiring
a whirl of smiles.

FAMILY ADVENTURES

Sometimes all my uncles decide
to explore the countryside, so we ride,
bumping and swaying in an old oxcart,
with rough cowhides forming a cover
to protect all my many cousins
from the fiery blaze of sun.

When I remember the cattle that guarded me
after I was stranded by my mother, I think I'd rather
be burnt by light than continue to hide
beneath a slaughtered animal-friend's skin . . .

but *los primos* sing as we go,
thrilled to be on our way, no matter
how gruesome
our shelter.

As soon as we reach a river,
I rush to swim and daydream,
washing unwanted memories
away.

A FAMILY MYSTERY

Tío Manuel is the only uncle
who makes me feel uncomfortable.

There's something about his stare,
as if he finds my timid gaze fascinating.

When we're hiking in high mountains
on the slopes of a smoky volcano,
I have plenty of chances
to escape from him.

I can't stand the way he always asks
so many questions about my mother's
disappearance.

In the rainy green jungle, I try to stay far away
from his booming rifle, and at the seashore
I'd rather listen to my older cousins' horrifying
ghost stories.

Why does this one particular uncle
always make me feel so vulnerable?

FAMILY CAMPING

We sleep in huts
made of leafy green branches,
all the children sneaking out
at midnight
to chase red crabs,
watch enormous turtles,
and dream beneath
glowing stars
as they glide
across dark sky
forming the ancient shapes
of magnificent constellations—
a winged horse, a dolphin,
a dragon, the Milky Way.

Does that hunter made of stars
use his arrows to shoot ordinary deer,
or is he seeking treasures that no one on Earth
has ever imagined?

Maybe all he wants to chase is the glow
of his own heavenly surroundings.
Stories come easily
as I combine old fairy tales
with my own curious rush
of new visions.

While stargazing in the wilderness,
I remember the tales of *A Thousand and One Nights*,
and then I change them.

Don Quixote.
Spain's Golden Age poets.
Native Miskito legends.
All are fair game when it comes to hunting
for unwritten star wishes.

WITNESS

One night, I decide to leave the crowd
of noisy cousins behind, so that I can stargaze
alone, turning my view of the wild sky's
radiance
into new rhymes.

At the edge of a swamp, I stumble upon a scene
so shocking that I wonder if I'm dreaming.
Beside an oxcart, two men battle with machetes,
until the hand of one is sent flying into the dark air,
chopped off.

Should I tell anyone what I've seen,
or will sensible grown-ups refuse to listen
to this tale of a violent crime witnessed by a child?

Isn't the role of poets to pass along truths,
both gruesome and beautiful?

Yes, I'll have to tell, and maybe someday
I'll put the terrifying memory in writing as well.

SUFFERING

Those men who fought turn out to be friends,
but they drank so much rum that they forgot
about affection, and now the one
who maimed the other
must live with guilt
for the rest of his life.

Of all my rowdy uncles, Manuel is the only one
who drinks so wildly that it's easy to imagine
violence leading to horrible crimes
like severed hands.

Is that why he looks at me so strangely,
because he suspects I've decided to become
the emotional sort of poet who never ignores
injustice, but writes it into a truthful
music of wishes?

I'm only eleven years old,
but that's plenty of time
to grow, learn, and know
my own soul.

HURRICANE

Back at home, when an explosive tropical storm
strikes the town of León, courageous Bernarda
meets the attack of howling wind
and torrential rain
with peaceful palm fronds.

All my aunts gather to arrange green leaves
as decorations intended to protect walls and ceilings.
Then they weave leafy crowns to be worn
by singing children.

Feeling like a hero in an ancient story,
I wear my glorious leaf crown proudly,
while chanting prayers we've all memorized
precisely for these fights against the power
of a rebellious sky.

Words, my brave aunts insist,
are weapons more effective
than swords.

SCANDAL

Once the air is finally calm,
people at church grow angry.

In this city, we've always had a tradition
of writing notes to God, revealing secrets
which will be burned just as soon as the priests
finish praying about all our private letters
without reading a single word.

When I see Bernarda carefully folding
the paper that holds our family's confessions,
I wonder if her letter might include anything
about my mother's disappearance, or the identity
of my dead father.

We trust the priests.
They're kind men who give chocolates to children.
Nevertheless, in this case they turn out to be dishonest.
Someone catches them reading the whole town's
basket of notes, laughing and whispering
about our secret lives.
It's an offense so serious
that they are sent away,
leaving the children of our town
without chocolates
or trust.

I don't know which is worse,
my sudden awareness that grown-ups
know all sorts of devious secrets,
or my imagination,
which runs wild,
creating stories that might be
even more horrible
than those folded letters
filled with hidden truths.

When all the confessions are finally burned,
I gaze at the basket of ashes, still wondering
if the papery dust contains any tales
about my parents.

REBELLIOUS RHYMES

If priests can break rules, so can I.

Eleven syllables
followed by three.

Seven lines
or twenty.

I can write a poem
in any form, just by inventing
my own new lengths, shapes,
and styles.

No one can tell me how to think
or what to believe, now that I'm
finally
twelve.

ACROBATICS OF THE HEART

I fall in love!
Yes, I'm still just twelve, but maybe she's
not much older. . . .

Her name is Hortensia, and she's a performer
in a traveling circus, *una saltimbanqui,*
a high-wire trapeze artist
from North America.

I've always been told by teachers
that the United States is a huge place
filled with brutish politicians
who want to invade all the smaller nations
of Latin America, but Hortensia
has conquered me
with aerial somersaults
instead of bullets.

The entire circus is magnificent—magicians, musicians,
jugglers, galloping trick riders, strange sideshows,
bizarre animals, and Hortensia's
astonishing
acrobatic flips,
cartwheels,

and impossible leaps,
the high-rising flight
of a human
bird girl!

WHEN YOU'RE IN LOVE,
EVERY WORD IS MAGICAL

If I don't see my beloved's
acrobatic performance
and hear her voice
every day
for the rest of my life,
I feel certain
that my heart
will crack open
like that golden pomegranate
during Easter week,
and all my stormy verses
will shower down,
sinking into the depths
of dry earth,
broken,
buried.

TRICKSTER

I don't have enough money
to go to the circus every day,
so I have to dream up many
sneaky ways
to enter.

One evening, I carry a violin,
pretending to be one of the musicians.

The next afternoon, I haul a stack of papers
to make myself look like an official.

Finally, after much trial and error,
I discover that the clown loves poetry,
so now I simply trade
rhythmic verses
for tickets.

His favorites are the romantic rhymes,
which I imagine he will recite as if they
are his own heartfelt poems, whenever he
falls as deeply in love
as this hopeful
twelve-year-old
trickster.

Unable to imagine
life without the circus,
I audition, but my poet's body
fails to pass all the tests
for athletic talent,
and I end up facing
Hortensia's unbearable
departure.

FEELING WORTHLESS

The end of first love is a high-wire balancing
                                challenge

without
            any
                        training

or
      a
      net.

The circus won't let me be a runaway,
so when their caravan of aerial marvels
moves on,
I'm left here with nothing
but my toppled
tumbling
earthbound
sorrow.

FEELING WORTHY

The inspiration that came from my admiration
for a dramatic and beautiful foreign acrobat
now makes my lonely poems seem to glow.

Everyone around me
agrees that I've grown.

The field where that circus stood
is just a scattered mass of trampled grass,
and I have to go back to school,
but while I sit motionless,
forced to listen
to rigid grammar lessons,
my mind wanders through old rhymes,
trying them over and over again
in new patterns.

Yes, broken hearts have a purpose,
writing verses to comfort
others.

THE POET BOY

People call me *el niño poeta*,
a nickname that follows me wherever I go.

My first publication is a poem in a newspaper
on the occasion of the death of a friend's father.

Suddenly I'm famous
in all the nations of Central America.

So I let my hair grow long
like my *indio* ancestors,
and I tie it back in a ponytail,
think of myself as a rebel,
and eventually I make a point
of neglecting my studies,
especially mathematics.

I fight with boys,
flirt with girls,
and absolutely refuse
to listen to grown-ups.

How can Tía Bernarda continue to tell me
that she expects me to be an apprentice
to a tailor?

Why should I stitch
rich men's ugly suits
when I can weave
beautiful words
into a wealth
of useful verses?

A TERRIBLE SECRET
IS FINALLY REVEALED

One day, a neighbor invites me to meet
a black-clad woman who claims to be
my mother.

This lost-and-found Mamá gives me candy
and little gifts, even though I'm almost thirteen,
too old to be distracted by toys and treats.

I learn that she never died.
She simply chose to deceive me.
She didn't want me, but now she does.
Is it because I'm famous, and she imagines
riches?

Forgiveness is a question
I can't answer yet.

After all, how long will it take for her
to forgive herself—centuries,
millennia, eternity?

ONE SECRET LEADS TO ANOTHER

As soon as my mother vanishes again,
I ask myself how much Tía Bernarda knew,
and why she and El Bocón never told me,
and yes, of course, naturally, next I must ask
my aunt:
>Is my father
>alive
>too?

VICIOUS NIGHTMARES ATTACK ME

Each hour of darkness
    is a dreaded pit of rage,
fueled by this new knowledge
    that, yes, Papá is alive
and I already know him;
    in fact, I detest him!

I am the son of Uncle Manuel
the drunkard.

No wonder we've always looked at each other
with such utter loathing and suspicion.

By day, I go to his fancy shop just to stare.
Why confront him, what would I say?

After sunset, I suffer alone
    unable to sleep
without dreaming
    of a faceless
armless
    footless
pale spirit
that reaches for me,
        its touch just as alarming
as the zigzag embrace
        of a jolting lightning ray,

electric
        scalding
sulfur-scented
                with a taste
                    like oily candle wax
            whenever I kick and bite,
                trying to fight back
            protecting myself
from the sadness
        of an evil
dream.

AFTER BETRAYAL

At sunrise, nightmares vanish,
replaced by Bernarda's fearsome stories
about my mother's brothers—Ignacio,
who was shot in a duel, and Antonio, dragged
behind a horse during a revolution.

Apparently, my family's history
was always riddled by tragedies.

Mamá married Manuel and divorced him
before I was born, because of his drunkenness,
but then he married one of my aunts, and now
I must live with his disturbing presence
as well as the hideous memory
of my mother's absence.

Perhaps it's better to claim no parents
than two who have no use for a son.

No matter how hard it seems,
I'll need to find some way to forgive
Bernarda for keeping such deeply
wounding
secrets.

If she hadn't adopted me,
I might now be
a wild child
raised by cattle.

DREAMS OF ESCAPE

Restless.
Desperate.

Something inside my mind is turning me into
a wanderer, bitter and distant.

It seems so natural now
to think of myself as homeless.

What comfort is there in the dull articles
I sell to newspapers, trying to earn money
to help the woman I thought of as a mother
for so many years, when all along, Bernarda knew
that my true Mamá
was alive and had no wish
to know me, while the father
I despise
was even
worse.

IMPERFECT POETRY IS MY ONLY REFUGE

The blue peace of sky.
Wings.
A view of passing birds.
Joy.
I try, but resentment
is determined to invade
my verses.

Forgiveness.
Not for my real parents,
no.

Maybe someday, after I've seen
this wide world's wonders,
just like the wanderer, El Bocón.

In the meantime, I use my written voice
loudly, scribbling protests against every
injustice, especially crimes
of personal, emotional, selfish
betrayal.

FRAGMENTS

No sorrow
is ever great enough
to destroy
nature's comforts,
so I manage
to salvage
slivers
of happiness
by rowing
up and down the jungled coast
alone in a small boat, passing through marshes
and tangled mangrove swamps, as I watch the ocean
where ships steam away
toward distant lands.

The sea is beautiful, and the breeze
brings a scent of forest flowers.

My horizon is vast, a limitless universe
of future verses.

SONGS OF LIFE

Thirteen is an age
of anticipation.

Soon I'll be a grown man,
ready for travel
and love.

Whenever I see a statue in the park
I imagine that it might
spring to life,
reversing the process
that preserves old soldiers
as rigid sculptures.

Then I scribble an eerie tale
at midnight—I am the block of marble
carved
and waiting
for tomorrow.

FOURTEEN

I find work teaching grammar, and writing
for a newspaper called *La Verdad*—The Truth.

But truth is never popular
with corrupt leaders
who rely
on lies.

So when the government disapproves
of my writing, I lose all desire to do anything
but listen.

I sit on the street beside Manuelita—a woman
who sells cigars—while she tells stories
of flying horses, magical genies,
and endless mazes
     where ancient heroes
         were always
wandering
   ending up

lost.

Manuelita's little dog
pays attention to these stories,
and then he listens intently

to my improvised verses
about the same myths.

The dog is called Laberinto,
even though Labyrinth sounds
like a concept too complex
for his wagging tail
and friendly eyes.

I'm already a failure
as a reporter, so how long
will it be
    until I find
           my own
pathway
           through
life's
    tangled
mazes?

MELANCHOLY

Sorrow transforms me.
I feel as if an invisible hand
is pushing me toward
the unknown ...

but people who come to León
for a glimpse of the famous Poet Boy
are never disappointed.

I'm always ready to entertain them
with passionate verses.

There is no greater inspiration
than sadness, but *ay, Dios*, my God,
how willing I would be
to trade
this sense
of uselessness
for travel, any adventure, a hopeful voyage
like the ones I used to read about in the shade
of my beloved gourd tree
and pomegranate.

AN INVITATION

Senators come to León
just to hear the Poet Boy
read a hurricane of verses.

When I finish the performance
they invite me to visit Managua,
the capital city of Nicaragua,
and now all my daydreams
of roaming
are suddenly
real!

MOVING AWAY FROM HOME

I feel winged.
Sunlight fills my breath, my lungs. . . .

I'm as blessed as one of Victor Hugo's
desolate characters in *Les Misèrables*,
a poet-witness accepted by influential men
despite my vast range of past failures.

I leave with Bernarda's blessing,
but soon, as I pass the peaceful blue waters
of Lake Xolotlán
and the fuming volcano
called Momotombo,
I begin to wonder
if my small-town rhymes
will ever be eloquent enough
for city dwellers . . .

but I'm fifteen years old, with a star
of hope clasped in my hand, so I keep my eyes
lifted toward the future's
limitless sky.

A CELEBRITY

How could I have known
that I would already be so famous,
paraded at parties and official banquets,
where elegant ladies constantly ask me
to write original poems
on their fancy silk fans?

Sonnets about their beauty—
I imagine that's what they expect,
and sometimes it's the sort of verse
I'm able to produce on short notice,
but there are other days
when all I want to say
is *la verdad*—the truth,
serving as history's
honest witness.

AN ACT OF CONGRESS

The senators vote about my future,
deciding to send me to France.

In Paris, I will receive
such a dreamlike education,
studying with Europe's greatest
masters of poetry!

All those years ago during Easter week
when I saw my own childhood verses
raining down from a golden pomegranate,
there was no way to foresee
this new shower
of generous
blessings.

DISAPPOINTMENT

The president of the republic
destroys all hope for a state-funded education.
He uses his veto power to deny the act of congress
that passed in my honor.

He calls my poetry insulting,
even though the verse he objects to
is just a parable about an angry ruler
who smashes his crown against a throne.

Yes, of course I'll continue to criticize
foolish leaders wherever I find them.

That's a decision I made at the edge of a swamp,
when I saw a man's severed hand flying.

Poets must speak, no matter the punishment.
We are observers with musical voices, testifying
in the courtrooms
of nature
and human life.

A WORLD OF BOOKS

Stranded in this hectic city,
I have to find a job, so I decide to apply
to the National Library, and even though
I'm so young, librarians accept me into their treasury
of ancient thoughts and modern ones.

Verses from so many nations!
Fables, myths, fantasies, translations!
Greeks and Romans
along with Aztecs and Mayas.
The wisdom of so many civilizations
swirls and blends, entering my imagination
through tangled gateways.
Why shouldn't my poetry feature Pegasus
alongside Quetzalcoatl?

My ancestry is both Spanish
and *indio*,
so my *mestizo* mind embraces
the mixture.

INDEPENDENT THOUGHT

The library's silence is mysterious.
Each book offers a gift of possibilities.

Soon I'm writing while I read,
combining my own endless
sense of wonder
with all the marvels
already told in astonishing stories
from history, sagas of travel, nature,
families, conflict, and love,
always love. . . .

Days pass, weeks, months.
There's nothing to stop me
from spending a lifetime
immersed in this endless
exploration
of pages, unless . . .

FALLING IN LOVE IS A CLIFF

n

o

t

a

s

l

o

p

e.

As soon as I've plummeted, I feel certain
that everyone will disapprove, because
she's so young too, and all we want
is to be married right away.
No reason to wait.
Grown-ups can't
stop
us.
Can they?

THIS FLURRY OF VERSES

Passionate love poems fly from my pen,
published in newspapers, so that even strangers
will know
how much I love her,
the girl with green eyes,
cinnamon skin, dazzling laughter,
and a magical voice that can sing any
enchantment.

In a garden of blue butterflies
and flowering flame trees
we stargaze
together.

Clasped hands.
Absolute silence.
    First
    kiss!

UNCERTAINTY

What if she doesn't really love me enough
to accept my proposal?

How can I wait years and years to get married,
until we're both older, wiser, and so much more
boring?

SELFISHNESS

A friend falls ill.
My beloved carries medicine
to his bedside.

Instead of sympathy for a sick young man's suffering,
all I feel is this frenzy of envy, as if love
has changed me
into the monstrous beast
called jealousy.

TORMENT

Unreasonable, that's what I am,
just a teenage poet boy,
unrealistic, greedy, maybe even
truly mean.

No one could be more cruel to me
than I am being to myself.

Where are all those bossy grown-ups now
when I suddenly need
their wisdom?

NATURE

I stand at the edge of a blue lake
alone.

Above me
white clouds and herons soar
toward some great unknown
heaven . . .

while down here, doves flutter,
wings swiftly entering my thoughts, filling me
with a restlessness
    that somehow
        eventually
           floats
              toward
                peace.

A DECLARATION OF LOVE

When I announce my intentions,
all my older friends laugh, slap me on the back,
and shake their heads with disbelief.

Poets, editors, librarians, even senators,
all share the same disturbing idea that marriage
is hard work, and must be reserved for mature,
educated, responsible adults.

Maybe they're right, but I won't soon find out
because they take up a collection, everyone
donating coins to buy me a ticket that they say
will carry me away to another country
where I'll have to stay until I'm older
and calm.

MISUNDERSTOOD

Adults think they understand everything,
while I don't know if I'll ever comprehend
anything.

If marriage is only meant for grown-ups,
why do teenagers always feel
so lovesick?

Shouldn't there be some easy way
to make passion
patient?

There is one approach, I suppose,
by pouring
all my stormy
thoughts and feelings
into poetry. . . .

A MOB OF GROWN-UPS

Friends
pack my bag
drag me to the port
push me onto a ship
and send me away
from the daydream
called love.

EXILE

From the deck of the ship
I see a port—La Libertad, El Salvador.

Now that I'm in a foreign country
where I know no one, what should I do,
try to make my way back across the border
toward memories of childhood,
or stay here and beg strangers
for help?

I DARE MYSELF

Courage
is a challenge.

So I'll meet it.
I must—I will!

Believing that I was an orphan
for so many years before learning the truth
about my devious parents
has made me accustomed
to expecting rejection,
but now—instead of
allowing myself
to feel only fear,
I claim a blaze
of confidence
as strong as one
of El Bocón's
bold stories.

Yes, I seize the bravest action I can think of,
relying on my imagination for guidance.
Courageously, I step off the ship
and find an office where I can send
a courteous telegram
to the powerful president
of El Salvador.

I call myself the Poet Boy
of Central America,
using fame as a bridge
between nations.

UNEXPECTED SUCCESS

The answer comes quickly.
A hearty welcome, and an invitation.
A driver.
A coach.
Horses.

Soon I'm on my way
to the capital city's
best hotel, with fine meals,
dazzling opera singers,
and a chance to visit
the presidential palace.

Apparently my reputation as *el niño poeta*
extends far beyond the borders of Nicaragua.

MEETING ANOTHER POWERFUL MAN

Surrounded by guards,
I can't admit that I'm heartsick,
love-torn, homesick, lonely . . .

so we speak of verses, the president expressing
his admiration for my poetry.

Then he asks: *¿Qué deseas?*
What do you wish?

This surprising question makes me hesitant.
I long to tell the truth about the green-eyed girl
and my dream of immediate marriage,
but I fear the same reaction I encountered before
among poets and senators—insulting laughter.

So what should a poet boy request?
Una buena posición social, I venture timidly,
imagining that "a good social position" will change
adult minds about everything else, because wealth
is so often mistaken for wisdom.

A GIFT OF RICHES

Long-haired and skinny,
I return to the fancy hotel
with five hundred silver coins,
a present from the president.

I feel as fortunate and overwhelmed
as a poor shepherd boy in a fairy tale,
but in those stories there is always a set
of three impossible tasks.

So what will the president demand
in return—verses in his honor?

What if I fail?

This isn't a magical world.
The tests will be challenges
to my character, not spells
cast by witches.

WASTED WEALTH

I fail so swiftly!
How easy it is to spend,
when plenty of local poets flock to greet me,
and I meet so many other friendly people,
the hotel such an easy place to celebrate
by ordering fancy food and drinks for all.

Ever since I learned that Uncle Manuel
is really my father, I've wondered whether I will
turn out to be a drunkard too.

Apparently I already am.
Too much rum, all the money gone,
raucous fights,
wild behavior,
until I find myself
evicted,
escorted
out the door
by a stern
police chief.

PUNISHMENT

Instead of the good social position
I wished for, suddenly I'm a prisoner.

The angry police chief
delivers me to a school
where he informs me
that by order
of the president
of El Salvador,
I must stay off the streets
and serve my sentence
by teaching grammar.

Estoy perdido.
I'm lost.

For how long will I have to recite
memorized rules, instead of writing
my own free truths?

THE STUDENTS ARE MY OWN AGE

What can I teach
that won't put them to sleep?

We work on irregular verbs, conjugations,
and punctuation, until finally I make up my mind
to experiment.

First, I try hypnosis,
an entertainment I learned
at the circus.

Next comes love letters, because of course
nothing else fascinates boys my age more
than girls, and nothing pleases a young girl
more than verses, especially
when the poems
are framed
within formal
gardens of prose.

Learning grammar is easy for students
who treasure an amorous goal.

TRULY A PRISON

Some schools only seem to have walls,
but here
the director never allows me to leave
for nine
entire months.

IN PRAISE OF FREEDOM

Time passes as slowly
as all the centuries of history,
but love letters are perfected,
and students receive glowing grades.

When the president hears reports
of my success as a teacher, he invites me
to write an elegant poem for a centennial celebration
in honor of Simón Bolívar, courageous liberator
of most of the Américas.

Second chances are rare blessings,
and I know that if I fail, I might end up
teaching grammar forever, so I make
an honest effort to praise liberty,
wrapping my rhymes and rhythms
in a veil of hope as peaceful
as blue sky
and blue sea.

A DIFFERENT KIND OF LIBERTY

The Bolívar centennial
means temporary liberation
from my prison, the school.

A dramatic recitation, then a fiesta,
such a wonderful party, where once again
I fall in love with a girl
my own age.

I set a table with a dinner
for invisible guests—Homer,
Pindar, and Virgil
from the ancient world,
and Cervantes, the author
of *Don Quixote*.

Then I offer a toast to each,
until I'm so drunk that I might as well be
a knight on a horse, challenging a windmill
to a duel, as if it were truly a giant with enormous
spinning
swords. . . .

I AM MY OWN PRISONER

Oh, why did I drink so much,
wasting precious freedom
and condemning myself
to adult disapproval?

Falling in love
made me foolish.

Toasting dead poets
led to drunkenness.

Now I'll have to face
the fury
of a president,
but first . . .

SMALLPOX

Oozing sores, pain, fear. . . .

Horror of scars, probably blindness,
the possibility of death. . . .

Passionate letters are set aside
half-finished.

By the time this unforeseen ordeal is finally over,
I find it impossible to believe that I ever craved
wealth, praise, or fame, when clearly
all that matters in life
are love
and health,
two treasures worthy
of celebration.

THE MATHEMATICS OF ANGER

Powerful men can do anything they want,
even when it means listening to gossip.

Rumors of wild celebrations are all it takes
for *el presidente* to send me away, back
to my own nation, the famous Poet Boy
shamed,
disgraced.

I've been abandoned by two parents,
hated by two presidents, and banished twice
just to keep me separated
from girls
who love
verses.

So my rage at authority doubles,
and my devotion
to rebellious poetry
multiplies.

WAITING TO GROW UP

Apparently while I was gone,
my death from smallpox was announced
in the newspaper, so when I reappear,
Bernarda and all my family and friends
are so relieved that they forgive
the rumors of my scandalous
behavior.

By now, Nicaragua has a new president
who grants me a dull secretarial job
that allows plenty of free time
for writing poems and stories.

What is there to say about feeling suspended
between childhood and maturity?

Each day is a road of dreams
leading toward my future—adult liberty.

LOVELESS IN MY OWN HOMELAND

On warm nights, I lie down
on a wooden dock beside the lake,
free to stargaze while I listen
to the music of rhythmic waves.

Daydreams and wishes,
hikes up steep volcanic slopes,
afternoons bird-watching,
evenings observing
turtles, monkeys,
fishermen, farmers,
and crocodile hunters.

What next?
Will I always spend
all my hours alone,
collecting visions, words,
rhythms, and melodies
for my solitary
whirlwind
of verses?

WRITING, WRITING, WRITING

I'm lonely, so I pass the time by practicing
imitations of French styles, Cuban ones,
and those of ancient Greeks.

In one poem, I mimic the verses
of fifteen different classical Spanish poets,
and I do it so expertly that every critic
can identify the masters I've chosen
as my long-dead guides.

I memorize dictionaries, both Spanish and Galician.
Then I translate French poems, and those written
by Miskito people from the Caribbean coast,
their native language a treasure to me,
not an embarrassment, the way so many
arrogant poets who only appreciate Europe
might assume.

BARS

Drinking
too much
jumbles
my verses.

Will I ever learn
to control
this
curse?

The poems I scribble
when I'm drunk
just sound like foolish
self-pity.

WHEN I'M SOBER

Terza rima, hendecasyllabic,
a style of three-lined stanzas
where each middle line rhymes
with the first and third lines
of the next tercet.

No poetic form is too complex.
I am determined to always claim
freedom
for experimentation . . .

but I still love wildly shaped verses too,
and imaginative stories told in prose,
with hurricanes of words
about the world,
not just my own
explosive
emotions.

WANDERLUST

Months pass, then years.
Life is restful, but soon enough
I begin to imagine adventures.

A new start, far away, perhaps even
the United States . . .

it's the country that produced William Walker,
a madman who tried to conquer Nicaragua,
but it's also the birthplace of so many poets:
Emerson
Whitman
Poe. . . .

Ever since my mother left me
in that cattle pasture, I've felt like a wanderer,
homeless.

Now I dream of roaming in a new way,
voluntarily, instead of by abandonment.

FINALLY

For a poet born in poverty,
the most likely way to have a book published
is by order of the government.

Now, it's happened, the president of Nicaragua
has decided to support me, so a volume
of my verses
will be printed,
almost
a miracle!

THE SOUL OF A POEM

All my older friends tell me
that as soon as my book is printed,
I must forget the distant United States
and sail in the opposite direction, to Chile,
the wealthiest nation of Latin America,
where every poet is published in Spanish.

The life of a verse, they insist, is found
in its original language, no matter how universal
the emotions.

Only a truly brilliant translator
can carry the glowing heart of a poem
from one word to another.

I am like a fish, my friends assure me
that can never be safely moved
from a freshwater tropical river
to any salty northern sea.

THE EDGE OF THE EARTH

I'm practically an adult now,
but when I think of distance
I feel small.

Chile lies at the southernmost tip
of South America,
thousands of miles away, reached only
by enduring
a long voyage on the ocean.

No matter how beautiful and musical
the waves are, I'll still be seasick
and isolated.

The mere thought
of such a challenging journey
makes me wistful for my childhood home
in León.

Wanderlust
is a powerful force
that leaves the eager traveler
longing to live
two lives
at the same time,
one of adventure,
the other
peace.

PREPARATIONS

A friend presents me
with letters of introduction
to a poet in Valparaíso
and a rich man in Santiago.

A collection is taken up,
until I hold a handful
of old Peruvian
gold coins.

I'll arrive in Chile with nothing
but paper, a pen, this bit of money,
and the star of hope that still
warms my hand . . .

but there will be no way
to make a living
if my flawed poems
are rejected
by editors
who expect
perfection.

WAR

Just when I'm finally ready to leave—
shouting
gunfire
rebellion!

All the separate republics
of Central America
launch a chaotic
jumble of battles.

New rulers
seize power.

Every moment of delay
is dangerous.

The journey I planned as an adventure
now turns into a desperate attempt
at escape . . .

but I'm too slow,
and before I have a chance
to flee
from this violent
man-made disaster,
nature reclaims
her absolute
authority.

EARTHQUAKE

Walls
    of a house
where
    I am visiting
crumble
    tumble
    fall.

Hopes in the mind where I thrive
give way to a crushing vigil
of
waiting
to find out
if I
will
survive.

But I'm not the only one trapped
by destruction.

A small child!
Instinctively,
I lift
my friend's daughter
and carry her
to safety

an act
that will forever
cause others to call me a hero
even though all I am is a weak man
who happens to be just a tiny bit bolder
than this thankfully smiling
five-year-old
girl.

My heart is changed
by the experience of helping.

None of the books I've read by Spanish, Cuban,
French, Greek, and North American poets
ever prepared me for the depth
of my new gratitude
to heaven
and earth.

VOLCANO

The era of natural disasters has not ended!
Fiery
    rivers
        of rolling
            lava
            flow
        down
    from
heights
    burying forests
            farms
     villages
            dreams....

Gray ash rains over the city, a torment
of horrors.

THE SUN DISAPPEARS

Lanterns are needed even at noon.
People move through a dusty gloom
of ashes and soot, our prayers rising
as we sing in the streets, all together,
everyone expecting sudden doom.

If this combination of war
followed by earthquakes
and a volcanic eruption
is not the end of the world,
then it must be a new beginning
of brotherly love, as everyone joins
our united effort to find survivors.

We succeed, but the government's print shop
has been destroyed.

There will be no published book of my poems,
just these scribbled papers, my treasury,
a battered suitcase
filled with verses.

YEARNING FOR LIGHT

If I were a bird
I'd rise above volcanic ashes
and soar far beyond this burning earth . . .

but I'm human,
so I use my shaky legs
to stumble through dark streets
searching for survivors
other poets
my friends.

Go to Chile,
they urge me
when we finally
locate each other.

Go, they repeat, flee, *niño poeta,*
try to reach the end of the earth,
even if you
have to swim,
even if you drown.

FLIGHT

After saying farewell to Bernarda,
I rush
to the docks
see a boat
buy a ticket
climb on board
steam away!

Am I really the only passenger?

The vessel turns out to be a German cargo ship.

No one on board speaks my language.

When I glance back at the shore
    I see my homeland
vanishing
    beneath swirling clouds
of dense
    smoke.

WONDERING

Am I a coward for leaving?
It will take my nation
and my family
many years
to recover
from so much damage.

I imagine these feelings
as one drop in a river,
the endless stream
of disasters,
both natural
and man-made.

Survivor's guilt
must always be
part of this rolling
wave of relief
felt by every
escaping
refugee.

LANGUAGE BARRIERS

An immense sorrow settles over me.
No one on the ship speaks Spanish
and I don't know any German, so I try
to communicate by using bits of English
that I've learned by reading translations
of North American poetry,
but the crew members don't
understand me, so we fall
into a pattern
of silence.

This loss of words
must be the first shock
faced by every immigrant.

A TRAVELER'S MIND

The sea is peaceful
and my dreams are invisible,
both future and past hidden
by distance.

Waiting
is the only way of life that exists now,
slow days spent watching waves,
then
endless nights
gazing up at starlight.

Each shorebird that soars above us,
leads my old pen toward new verses.

TRAVELING WITH
INVISIBLE MENTORS

I love the writing of Cuba's José Martí
and France's Victor Hugo,
but I need
my own style, so I scribble
aboard this ship of daydreams,
steaming alone
toward my future.

UN AMIGO

One friend is enough.
The captain smiles,
wordlessly inviting me
to play dominoes.

We eat in his cabin.
I learn a few words of German.
When we stop at ports, I see how little is needed
to make poor people happy.

In forests, there are clearings where children play.
In stark deserts, the only trees and flowers
are painted on walls, lush green murals
that create a satisfying illusion
of abundance.

WHEN I WRITE POETRY

Time on the ship passes slowly and swiftly
at the same time, a mystery of syllables,
silences,
and rhyme.

I discover the beauty of waves
that come
and then go again, in patterns of long
and short
tidal rhythms.

When I experiment with a variety of styles
certain verses end up seeming as wide as the ocean
which pulls seawater back and forth so furiously
that even the brave
restless moon
follows.

I've given up the idea of home—all I have now
are dreams, and this need to roam.

NINETEEN YEARS OLD

I'm like the roaming moon,
ready to face anything,
such a wealth of wonders
and painful frustrations
that the strange future
of every wanderer
brings.

IMAGINARY ORCHARDS

Quietly, I remember my childhood
of peaceful days spent reading
between the gourd tree
and the pomegranate.

Then I think of Easter week, and the way
a single, gleaming golden fruit exploded,
releasing seeds for the growth
of my smallest poems.

If I don't find a publisher in Chile,
then I'll just keep writing anyway,
serving as my own audience
for honest verses.

I feel like a hunter of daydreams,
armed with nothing but hours
vowel rhymes
and truth.

A FOREIGNER AT THE
END OF THE EARTH

The ship finally steams
into the glorious port of Valparaíso.

The first thing I do is buy a newspaper,
feeling stunned by the reality
of arrival.

The leading story of the day
is about the death of a famous historian
whose books I know well, so I spend
twenty minutes
scribbling my own
analysis of his work.

With this article and my suitcase
full of poems, I have all the luggage
I'll ever need.

FINDING MY WAY

Which hotel?
It's the same dilemma I faced
when I was exiled to El Salvador.

A shabby room is all I can afford,
but a pianist who is staying at the same inn
makes our surroundings seem elegant
as he sends festive music
rising up into the air.

Creativity is the best fuel
for every poor man's future.

As soon as I'm settled,
I take my article about the historian
to a newspaper office, where the friendly editor
accepts my work, and pays me generously.

Even the tiniest bit of encouragement
is enough to make an ordinary poet
feel truly heroic!

JUDGED

A new friend from the newspaper
helps me send my letter of introduction
to the rich man in Santiago,
the biggest city in Chile.

Soon I'm on my way, seated on the train,
wondering why so many gentlemen and ladies
frown and whisper, glaring at me
with disgust.

Un indio.
I hear the murmurs.

My brown skin.
Long hair.

Mended clothes.
Broken shoes.

Bursting suitcase.
Dream-filled gaze.

REFUSING TO BE JUDGED

In my homeland, I was just one
of thousands of *mestizos*, but here
so many people have only Spanish blood,
and anti-indigenous racial hatred
strikes my life
for the first time.

Los indios are the conquered,
while descendants of colonial Spaniards
continue to think of themselves as superior,
even though many decades have passed
since the hero Simón Bolívar
freed everyone
equally.

Let these pale people who think
they're so much better
judge me by my words
and actions
not
my skin.

ACCEPTING MY SELF

I become determined
to mix the ancient myths of Greece
with native Aztec and Maya images
from various nations of *las Américas*.

Chile has other aspects
that are new to me too,
such as seasons of cold,
not just the equally hot
wet and dry months
that I know
from the tropics.

I'm the only one on this train
without a warm jacket.

Let them stare at me.
Pretty soon I'll freeze
and all they'll see
is an icy skeleton.

ANGER IS NATURAL

It's easy to speak of defiance, but the truth is
that I feel defeated and desperate.

Inside my old suitcase,
a storm of verses is hidden.

With paper as my sky, words
are the wind that should help my mind fly.

If only my heart could follow,
celebrating any chance to transform
life's hardships
        into rhythmic artworks,
like the desert people
        who paint murals
of flowering green forests
        on barren
adobe walls.

For now, this drumbeat of rage
will be my only poetry.

BUZZING BEES OF HOPE

At the train station in Santiago, I turn away
from the disdainful faces of those who judge me,
while all around us, families embrace, reunited.

Joyful cries, food vendors, the rush of porters
carrying luggage . . .

I stand alone, waiting, until finally I see a carriage
with fancy horses, a driver in his elegant uniform,
and a valet who helps a wealthy man
step down
to search
for the person
he's meeting.

He's wrapped in luxurious furs.
Could this be the rich man who received
my letter of introduction?

When we are the only two people left
on the platform, he approaches me
and asks if I might happen to be
the famous Rubén Darío,
el niño poeta.

Yes, I'm the celebrated Poet Boy
but what does that even mean
now that I'm a grown man of nineteen?

My childhood verses were just practice
for the way I plan to write now, whenever
a stranger judges me as anything less
than an angry hive filled
with the hopeful bees
of equality.

A ROOM AT THE END
OF THE EARTH

I enter my new life
with a wealth of ideas
instead of money and clothing.

I have a place to stay, and I'm given a job
at a newspaper, but I feel so timid
each time I'm surrounded
by wealthy men
who think of me
as a poor *indio*.

Is envy part of the problem?
Does the fame that precedes me
lead them to expect someone who looks
powerful, wearing the latest fashions
from Paris, and writing in a more
conventional style?

WHEN I'M ASKED TO DESCRIBE
THE PROCESS OF WRITING

I simply tell the truth,
even though so many skeptics
don't find it easy to believe.

My poems are born whole
after long moments of concentration,
the first drafts unwritten, hidden deep within
the silent confines
of my mind.

POETRY WINGS

Eventually, I meet a few friendly people
who understand my shyness.

There is a young man my age
who is often ill, so he has sympathy
for my homesickness.

His father turns out to be
the president of Chile,
who invites me to lunch,
where I'm treated
like family.

When I win a verse competition,
I'm surprised, but all the other guests
say they expected it.

Triumph is a feeling like flight,
a hopeful unfolding of feathers,
and then the sheer delight
of feeling accepted.

REJECTION

Back in Valparaíso, I find work
at the customs office, keeping track
of goods that arrive and depart on ships.

Boxes.
Bundles.
Sacks of grain.
Did I really win
a poetry competition?

Boring work leaves my mind free
to dream up articles that might be of interest
to newspapers.

When I write about sports, I'm told
that I express myself too clearly.

It's not what we need, the editor informs me.
Those are the words every writer dreads,
but discouragement is never an option,
we all have to keep scribbling, or our voices
will vanish.

PERSEVERANCE

All my thoughts are a mixture
of swift disappointments
and endless efforts.

I stay away from work
more often than I go in.

Excuses make me feel ashamed,
but I pretend to be sick, just so I can be free
to stroll along the shoreline, boarding small boats
to go exploring.

The sea
is beautiful,
and my dreams
are invisible,
but my pen
is strong
and persistent.

I never give up
the flow of poems
aimed at waves
and wind.

Mind storms.
Verse hurricanes.

Stories about gnomes, nymphs,
and palaces of sunlight,
the tale of a man who keeps
a bluebird trapped within the cage
of his mind, even though the poor creature
yearns to be free, soaring alone in endless sky.

I write about verses brought to earth
by dark *garzas*, the graceful herons
that fly above me each time I go out
exploring.

I write about Chile's changing seasons,
and Nicaragua's tropical blossoms,
about every aspect of nature
and human nature,
then I add a fantasy
about the queen of fairies,
who travels in a pearl
pulled by golden beetles.

In this story of long ago,
there was a time when everyone
received a magical gift, either riches, strength,
eagle wings, harmony, rhythm, a rainbow,
sunlight, the melodies of stars,
or the music of jungles . . .

but humans envied each other's gifts,
bickering and battling, so that now
all of us are always granted the same wish,
receiving only a peaceful blue veil of dreams
for the future—in other words, nothing
but hope.

DANGER

Sometimes on quiet evenings
I visit hillside villages.

The music of poor men comforts me.
Days spent tunneling underground
must be so dark and harsh, but outdoors
at night, miners fill the village air
with songs of light . . .

until guitar players and singers
are surrounded
by drinkers,
and fights break out,
guns are drawn,
shots fired,
people injured.

When I accompany a doctor
to the bedside of a wounded man,
it feels oddly familiar
to once again be
a witness,
an outside observer
possessing no weapons
just verses
mere words.

This could have been me, lying bleeding
and helpless, back when I was younger
and more reckless, drinking, fighting,
and rebelling against the whole world
instead of just speaking out against
injustice.

At dawn, I leave the hills,
my heart filled with wonder
at the way human voices
persist in singing to blue sky,
no matter how crushing
the poverty, no matter
how dark
the tunnels
where miners
are forced to labor,
their suffering constantly
interrupted by daydreams.

NO LONGER A TEENAGER

I'm hired by *La Nación*, the same famous
Argentine newspaper that publishes my hero,
José Martí, the Cuban poet I think of as a mentor
even though I've never met him.

My editor wants one new poem each day.
It seems impossible, but I'm sure I can do it,
if I keep reading the verses of others, to find
inspiration.

Martí praises freedom, equality, and hope.
I treasure the same themes, but everyone says
that my style is completely new, musical rhythms
filled with colors that resemble paintings
by impressionists, the sentences in prose poems
made short, simple, and visual
by my love of art
and love of love.

MY FIRST BOOK

Azul.
Blue.
The calm title shows
how my hurricane of verses
helps me find
a sea
of peace.

A LIFETIME OF REBELLIOUS
RHYTHMS AND RHYMES

Travels to many lands,
marriage, babies, revolutions,
sorrows and joys, a meeting
with Martí in New York,
the inspiration to write
every day. . . .

In one verse, I warn Theodore Roosevelt,
powerful president of the United States,
that his aggressive nation's violent invasions
of Latin America
will be met with furious
resistance.

It's not difficult to predict wars
that are still far off in the distant future.
All the signs are present now—the US plans
to dominate our whole Spanish-speaking world.

They won't succeed, because we will refuse
to be ruled by arrogant racial hatred.

In Mexico, I offend the dictator Porfirio Díaz,
and in Cuba, I read my verses out loud
to crowds of humble farmers,

surrounded by their listening wives
and spellbound children.

After all my complex poems written for grown-ups,
I end up feeling surprised that my most prized
and beloved words
are those of a fairy tale
I scribbled on the fan
of a young girl
named Margarita.

The first stanza is about
the beautiful sea
and scented wind,
pleasing images which lead
to a story of rebellious
independence.

Princess Margarita defies her father
by flying up into the sky
to fetch a brilliant star.

When the angry king warns
that heaven will punish her,
God himself speaks, revealing
that He's pleased, admiring
her courage and perseverance
so sincerely

that He allows her
to carry the glittering treasure
back to Earth, where she wears
the star of light
as a jewel, fastened
to her silk clothing
right beside the rest
of her natural collection
of wonders—a feather,
a flower, a poem,
and a pearl.

MY MESSAGE FOR THE FUTURE

At first, I'm astonished by the popularity
of my most famous verse, but now I realize
that nothing means more to children
than hope—simply knowing they can grow up
and think for themselves, following the glow
of constellations
as they travel
beyond expectations,
to find peace
in a storm of dreams,
by reaching up to claim
the gleaming light
of their own star-bright
imaginations.

AUTHOR'S NOTE

I wrote this book because my Cuban ancestors were some of the humble farmers who attended poetry readings when Darío traveled to the island. Little did he know how inspiring his poetry would be for my great-grandmother and all her descendants. At family gatherings, Darío's verses were recited, just as I described in *The Wild Book,* a verse novel about my grandmother's childhood. In fact, the Nicaraguan poet was so revered in our family that two of my great-uncles were named Rubén and Darío in his honor, and I am not the first Margarita.

With a Star in My Hand is historical fiction based on the autobiography of Rubén Darío (1867–1916). All the events and situations are factual, and because Darío wrote so clearly about his childhood and youth, most of the emotional aspects are also taken from documented sources. Only a few small details have been imagined.

Darío is known as the Father of *modernismo*, a literary movement that blended poetry and prose, complex rhymes, assonance (vowel rhymes), and free verse, as well as classical European and indigenous Native American images. The 1888 publication of *Azul* in Valparaíso—when Darío was only twenty-one—is widely regarded as a revolutionary turning point in world literature. Until that time, romantic poetry tended to be overly sentimental, dwelling on one's own emotions instead of observing the entire world, with its interwoven array of troubles and beauty.

Darío's importance continued to grow throughout the first half of the twentieth century, and continues long after his death. His birthplace, the town of Metapa, is now called Ciudad Darío.

The National Library of Nicaragua was renamed in his honor. His childhood home in León is a museum visited by poets from all over the world.

As the early twentieth-century mentor of Juan Ramón Jiménez, Darío influenced Spain's Generation of 1927, a group of poets who spoke out against the fascist dictatorship of Franco. They included Federico García Lorca, Jorge Guillén, Pedro Salinas, and Rafael Alberti, who in turn influenced Mexico's Octavio Paz, Argentina's Jorge Luis Borges, Cuba's Alejo Carpentier, Chile's Pablo Neruda and Gabriela Mistral, and Colombia's Gabriel García Márquez. Unifying themes for all these writers are freedom, imagination, and the dream of social justice. It is a literary tradition that still thrives today, in the work of nearly every modern Latin American and US Latino poet and novelist.

Pablo Neruda described Darío as a sonorous elephant who shattered all the crystals of an era to let in fresh air. Pedro Salinas wrote that Darío was always half in this world and half out of it, a dreamy tendency which can be found in the work of all "magic realists," modern Latin America's answer to fantasy. Described in Spanish as *lo real maravilloso* (marvelous reality), magic realism shows ordinary lives touched by specific natural and supernatural marvels, rather than imagining completely separate alternate worlds.

After the publication of *Azul* in Chile, Darío returned to Nicaragua. He was received as a hero in León, but soon moved to El Salvador, where he became the director of a newspaper that promoted the unification of Central America as one country. Soon after he got married, he was forced to flee to Guatemala due to a military coup that overthrew the government of El Salvador. Over the next few decades, he lived in many countries, wrote for newspapers, published several poetry books, served as Nicaragua's ambassador to various countries, and was often impoverished.

Despite a stormy personal life and sophisticated literary body of work, Rubén Darío is most often remembered by the general public for his rhymed fairy tale, "A Margarita Debayle." He composed this long poem spontaneously, when the five-year-old daughter of a friend asked him to tell her a story.

"A Margarita Debayle" is so beloved in every Spanish-speaking country that it has been recited by parents and grandparents to the spellbound children of many generations. The story of a princess who flies to the sky to claim a star for herself was far ahead of its time, showing girls that they could be independent. "A Margarita Debayle" begins with an introduction that many Latino children know by heart:

> *Margarita, está linda la mar,*
> *y el viento*
> *lleva esencia sutil de azahar;*
> *yo siento*
> *en el alma una alondra cantar:*
> *tu acento.*
> *Margarita, te voy a cantar*
> *un cuento.*

Without attempting to reproduce the beautiful rhyme, assonance, and meter, the above stanza can be loosely translated as:

Margarita, the sea is beautiful,
and the wind
carries a subtle scent of orange blossoms;
I feel
a skylark singing in my soul:
your voice.
Margarita, I am going to tell you
a story.

To read the entire long poem in rhymed English, see Rosalma Zubizarreta's expert translation at the end of *Dancing Home* by Alma Flor Ada and Gabriel M. Zubizarreta (Atheneum, 2011).

REFERENCES

Darío, Rubén. *Autobiografía de Rubén Darío*. Barcelona: Red Ediciones, 2015.

Darío, Rubén. *Azul*. Buenos Aires: Editorial Sopena, 1947.

Darío, Rubén. *Prosas profanas*. Buenos Aires: Editorial Sopena, 1947.

Darío, Rubén. *Songs of Life and Hope/Cantos de vida y esperanza*. Durham, NC: Duke University Press, 2004.

Jiménez, Juan Ramón. *Mi Rubén Darío*. Madrid: Visor Libros, 2012.

Lázaro, Georgina. Ilustrado por Lonnie Ruiz. *Rubén Darío*. Lyndhurst, NJ: Lectorum, 2017.

Morrow, John A. *Amerindian Elements in the Poetry of Rubén Darío*. Lewiston, NY: Edwin Mellen Press, 2008.

Watland, Charles D. *Poet Errant, A Biography of Rubén Darío*. New York: Philosophical Library, 1965.